THE USBORNE
FIRST
THOUSAND
WORDS
IN JAPANESE
With easy pronunciation guide

Heather Amery
Illustrated by Stephen Cartwright
Revised edition edited by Nicole Irving
and designed by Andy Griffin

Japanese language consultants:
Joyce Jenkins, Tomoko Taguchi-Boyd and Kayoko Yokoyama
With thanks to Ian Way

About *kana* signs

The words in this book are written in simple Japanese signs, called *kana*. Each *kana* represents a syllable. (A syllable is part of a word that is a separate sound, for example, "today" has two syllables: "to" and "day".)

Below you can see all the *kana* signs and find out which sound they represent. There are also lots of tips to help you make these sounds like a Japanese person.

Japanese has two sets of *kana* signs. *Hiragana* signs are used for the traditional sounds of Japanese. *Katakana* signs are used for words that Japanese has borrowed from other languages, such as "taoru", borrowed from the English word "towel".

Next to each *kana*, you can see a guide to how it is said. In the book, each Japanese word is shown in the same way, that is, in *kana* with a pronunciation guide based on the guides on this page.

Hiragana

あ	a	い	i	う	u	え	e	お	o
か	ka	き	ki	く	ku	け	ke	こ	ko
が	*ga*	ぎ	*gi*	ぐ	*gu*	げ	*ge*	ご	*go*
さ	sa	し	shi	す	su	せ	se	そ	so
ざ	*za*	じ	*ji*	ず	*zu*	ぜ	*ze*	ぞ	*zo*
た	ta	ち	chi	つ	tsu	て	te	と	to
だ	*da*			づ	*zu*	で	*de*	ど	*do*
な	na	に	ni	ぬ	nu	ね	ne	の	no
は	ha	ひ	hi	ふ	fu	へ	he	ほ	ho
ば	*ba*	び	*bi*	ぶ	*bu*	べ	*be*	ぼ	*bo*
ぱ	*pa*	ぴ	*pi*	ぷ	*pu*	ぺ	*pe*	ぽ	*po*
ま	ma	み	mi	む	mu	め	me	も	mo
や	ya			ゆ	yu			よ	yo
ら	ra	り	ri	る	ru	れ	re	ろ	ro
わ	wa							を	(w)o
ん	n								

Katakana

ア	a	イ	i	ウ	u	エ	e	オ	o
カ	ka	キ	ki	ク	ku	ケ	ke	コ	ko
ガ	*ga*	ギ	*gi*	グ	*gu*	ゲ	*ge*	ゴ	*go*
サ	sa	シ	shi	ス	su	セ	se	ソ	so
ザ	*za*	ジ	*ji*	ズ	*zu*	ゼ	*ze*	ゾ	*zo*
タ	ta	チ	chi	ツ	tsu	テ	te	ト	to
ダ	*da*			ヅ	*zu*	デ	*de*	ド	*do*
ナ	na	ニ	ni	ヌ	nu	ネ	ne	ノ	no
ハ	ha	ヒ	hi	フ	fu	ヘ	he	ホ	ho
バ	*ba*	ビ	*bi*	ブ	*bu*	ベ	*be*	ボ	*bo*
パ	*pa*	ピ	*pi*	プ	*pu*	ペ	*pe*	ポ	*po*
マ	ma	ミ	mi	ム	mu	メ	me	モ	mo
ヤ	ya			ユ	yu			ヨ	yo
ラ	ra	リ	ri	ル	ru	レ	re	ロ	ro
ワ	wa							ヲ	(w)o
ン	n								

In the two lists above, the lines of slanted letters *(like these)* are based on the lines above them. As you can see, to make the new set of sounds, you just add a little mark to the top set of *kana* (ひ becomes び or ぴ).

Pronunciation tips

Here are a few tips that will help you to say the *kana* signs above in a really Japanese way.

Wherever the pronunciation guide shows **a**, say this like the "a" in "father";

say **i** like the "ee" in "meet";

say **u** like the "u" (or the "oo") in "cuckoo";

say **e** like the "e" in "end";

say **o** like the "o" in "corn".

When you see a line over a letter in the pronunciation guide (for example ō), this shows the sound is long.

For other letters, say them as if they were part of an English word, but remember these tips:

when you see **r**, say it as a soft "r" sound, halfway between an "l" and an "r";

when you see **g**, say it as in "garden";

the **(w)o** sound is shown with the "w" in brackets because you sometimes say "wo", and sometimes just "o". In this book, the pronunciation guide for each word will make it clear which sound to make;

the **fu** sound is halfway between "foo" and "hoo"

the **n** sound on its own (at the bottom of each list) is a nasal "n" sound, made as if you had a cold.

In English, many words have a part that you stress, or say louder. For example, in the word "daisy", you stress "dai". In Japanese, you say each part of the word with the same stress.

On every big picture across two pages,
there is a little yellow duck to look for.
Can you find it?

About this book

This book is for everyone who is starting to learn Japanese, and for anyone who wants to know something about the language. By looking at the small, labeled pictures, it will be easy to learn the words. You can also look at the large central picture and try to recall words for things. This helps words to stick in your mind, and it is also fun. Seeing things in a scene will also help you to remember them.

Looking at Japanese words

You will see that Japanese words are written with special signs. You can find out about these below and on the opposite page. It will take you a little time to learn Japanese signs, so to help you, each label in this book also shows the Japanese word in our alphabet.

Saying Japanese words

If you know someone who can speak Japanese, the best way to learn how to say Japanese words is to listen to them and repeat what you hear. To help you, though, throughout this book, you will find an easy how-to-say guide for each Japanese word. To be sure that you get the best results from these guides, look at the pronunciation tips on the opposite page.

Writing from right to left and top to bottom

Traditionally, Japanese is written from right to left and top to bottom. This means you start a book at what we call the back. In this book, everything is written from left to right, just as in English.

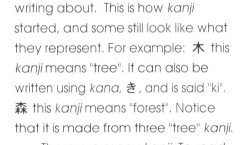

About *kanji*

The Japanese signs used in this book (see the page opposite) are called *kana*, and they are based on sounds. They are simple signs that you use when you first learn Japanese. Normally, they are used mixed in with some other, more complicated signs, called *kanji* or "characters". Each *kanji* represents a word or an idea.

When people first started to write, they used simple pictures of things to show what they were writing about. This is how *kanji* started, and some still look like what they represent. For example: 木 this *kanji* means "tree". It can also be written using *kana*, き, and is said "ki". 森 this *kanji* means "forest". Notice that it is made from three "tree" *kanji*.

There are many *kanji*. To read a newspaper, you have to know around 2000. It takes a few years to learn them, so it is best to start with *kana*, learning a few of these at a time.

おふろ ofuro

せっけん sekken

じゃぐち jaguchi

トイレット・ペーパー
toiretto-pêpâ

ハブラシ ha-burashi

みず mizu

トイレ toire

スポンジ suponji

せんめんだい senmendai

シャワー shawā

タオル taoru

うち uchi

ベッド beddo

よくしつ yokushitsu

いま ima

はみがきこ
hamigakiko

ラジオ rajio

クッション
kusshon

シーディー
shiidii

じゅうたん
jūtan

ソファー sofā

いす isu

かけぶとん kakebuton

くし kushi

シーツ shiitsu

しきもの shikimono

ようふくだんす
yōfuku-dansu

まくら makura

たんす tansu

かがみ kagami

ブラシ burashi

ランプ ranpu

え e

ぼうしかけ bōshi-kake

でんわ denwa

かいだん kaidan

しんしつ
shinshitsu

げんかん
genkan

 ラジエーター
rajiētā

 ビデオ bideo

しんぶん shinbun

 テーブル tēburu

 てがみ tegami

 かいだん kaidan

5

れいぞうこ reizōko

コップ koppu

とけい tokei

こしかけ koshikake

こさじ kosaji

スイッチ suitchi

せんざい senzai

かぎ kagi

ドア doa

だいどころ daidokoro

ながし nagashi

でんきそうじき
denki-sōjiki

なべ nabe

フォーク fôku

エプロン epuron

アイロンだい airon-dai

ごみ gomi

6

やかん yakan

ナイフ naifu

モップ moppu

はたき hataki

タイル tairu

ほうき hōki

せんたくき sentakuki

ちりとり chiritori

ひきだし hikidashi

うけざら ukezara

フライパン furaipan

レンジ renji

スプーン supūn

おさら osara

アイロン airon

しょっきだな
shokki-dana

ふきん fukin

コーヒーカップ
kōhii-kappu

マッチ matchi

たわし tawashi

おわん owan

じょうろ jōro

にわ niwa

ておしいちりんしゃ
te-oshi-ichirinsha

みつばちのす
mitsubachi no su

かたつむり katatsumuri

れんが renga

はと hato

すき suki

てんとうむし tentō-mushi

ごみいれ gomi-ire

たね tane

こや koya

みみず mimizu

はな hana

スプリンクラー
supurinkurā

くわ kuwa

すずめばち
suzume-bachi

8

みつばち mitsubachi

シャベル shaberu

ほね hone

かきね kakine

またぐわ mataguwa

しばかりき shibakariki

こみち ko-michi

は ha

き ki

けむり kemuri

けむし kemushi

くまで kumade

とりのす tori no su

ぼう bō

くさ kusa

うばぐるま ubaguruma

はしご hashigo

たきび takibi

ホース hōsu

おんしつ onshitsu

9

まんりき manriki

かみやすり kami-yasuri

ドリル doriru

はしご hashigo

のこぎり nokogiri

おがくず ogakuzu

カレンダー karendā

どうぐばこ dōgu-bako

さぎょうば sagyōba

ねじ neji

スクリュードライバー
sukuryū-doraibā

いた ita

かんなくず kanna-kuzu

ペンナイフ pen-naifu

びょう byō
くも kumo
ボルト boruto
おやねじ oya-neji
くものす kumo no su

たる taru
はえ hae
おの ono
まきじゃく makijaku
ハンマー hanmǎ
やすり yasuri
かんペンキ kan-penki
かんな kanna

ざいもく zaimoku
くぎ kugi
さぎょうだい sagyôdai
びん bin

とおり tōri

みせ mise

あな ana

きっさてん kissaten

きゅうきゅうしゃ kyūkyūsha

ほどう hodō

アンテナ antena

えんとつ entotsu

やね yane

しゅんせつき shunsetsuki

バス basu

ホテル hoteru

おとこ otoko

パトカー patokā

パイプ paipu

ドリル doriru

がっこう gakkō

うんどうじょう undō-jō

タクシー
takushii

おうだんほどう
ōdan-hodō

こうじょう kōjō

トラック torakku

こうつうしんごう
kōtsū-shingō

えいがかん eiga-kan

ライトバン raito-ban

ローラー rōrā

トレーラー torērā

いえ ie

いちば ichiba

ふみだん fumidan

オートバイ ōtobai

じてんしゃ
jitensha

しょうぼうしゃ shōbō-sha

けいかん keikan

くるま kuruma

おんな onna

がいとう
gaitō

アパート apāto

13

きしゃセット kisha-setto

さいころ saikoro

レコーダー rekōdā

ロボット robotto

ドラム doramu

ネックレス nekkuresu

カメラ kamera

ビーズ biizu

にんぎょう ningyō

ギター gitā

ゆびわ yubiwa

にんぎょうのいえ
ningyō no ie

おもちゃや omochaya

ハーモニカ hāmonika

ふえ fue

つみき tsumiki

おしろ o-shiro

せんすいかん sensuikan

トランペット
toranpetto

や ya

ゆみ yumi

パラシュート parashūto

ボート bōto

フェイスペイント fueisu-peinto

ローラー rōrā

おめん omen

レーシングカー rēshingu-kā

もくば mokuba

ちょきんばこ chokin-bako

ビーだま bii-dama

あやつりにんぎょう ayatsuri-ningyō

ピアノ piano

うちゅうひこうし uchū-hikōshi

クレーン kurēn

ねんど nendo

てっぽう teppō

へいたい heitai

えのぐ enogu

ロケット roketto

ぶらんこ buranko

すなば sunaba

ピクニック pikunikku

たこ tako

アイスクリーム
aisukuriimu

いぬ inu

もん mon

こみち ko-michi

かえる kaeru

すべりだい
suberidai

こうえん kōen

ベンチ benchi

おたまじゃくし
otamajakushi

いけ ike

ローラースケート rōrā-sukēto

やぶ yabu

あかんぼう
akanbō

スケートボード
sukētobōdo

つち tsuchi

ておしぐるま
te-oshi-guruma

シーソー shiisō

こども kodomo

さんりんしゃ sanrinsha

とり tori

さく saku

まり mari

ヨット yotto

いと ito

みずたまり mizu-tamari

こがも ko-gamo

なわとび nawatobi

き ki

かだん kadan

はくちょう hakuchō

ひきひも hikihimo

かも kamo

どうぶつえん dōbutsuen

つばさ tsubasa

わし washi

かば kaba

パンダ panda

ゴリラ gorira

まえあし mae-ashi

カンガルー kangarū

こうもり kōmori

さる saru

ひょうざん hyōzan

ペンギン pengin

しっぽ shippo

おおかみ ōkami

わに wani

くま kuma

はね hane

ペリカン perikan

だちょう dachō

イルカ iruka

ライオン raion

ようじゅう yōjū

キリン kirin

つの tsuno

しか shika

らくだ rakuda

あざらし azarashi

しろくま shiro-kuma

かめ kame

ぞうのはな zō no hana

さい sai

やぎゅう yagyū

ぞう zō

ビーバー biibā

やぎ yagi

しまうま shima-uma

へび hebi

さめ same

くじら kujira

とら tora

ひょう hyō

19

りょこう ryokō

せんろ senro

エンジン enjin

かんしょうき kanshōki

きゃくしゃ kyakusha

うんてんしゅ untenshu

かしゃ kasha

プラットフォーム puratto-hōmu

しゃしょう shashō

スーツケース sūtsukēsu

じょうしゃけんはんばいき jōshaken-hanbaiki

ヘリコプター herikoputā

えき eki

ガソリンスタンド gasorin-sutando

しんごう shingō

リュックサック rukkusakku

ヘッドライト heddo-raito

エンジン enjin

しゃりん sharin

でんち denchi

20

ひこうき hikōki

スチュワーデス suchuwādesu

かっそうろ kassōro

かんせいとう kanseitō

ひこうじょう hikōjō

スチュワード suchuwādo

パイロット pairotto

せんしゃ sensha

トランク toranku

ガソリン gasorin

レッカーしゃ rekkā-sha

せんしゃ

ガソリンタンクローリー gasorin-tankurōrii

スパナ supana

タイヤ taiya

ボンネット bonnetto

オイル oiru

ガソリンポンプ gasorin-ponpu

21

ふうしゃごや
fūsha-goya

ねつききゅう
netsu-kikyū

ちょうちょう chō-chō

とかげ tokage

いし ishi

きつね kitsune

おがわ ogawa

みちしるべ
michi-shirube

はりねずみ hari-nezumi

すいもん sui-mon

いなか inaka

やま yama

りす risu

もり mori

あなぐま anaguma

かわ kawa

みち michi

テント tento

うんが unga

まるた maruta

むら mura

が ga

はし hashi

はしけ hashike

たき taki

ふくろう fukurō

トンネル tonneru

こぎつね kogitsune

もぐら mogura

つりびと tsuri-bito

いわ iwa

ひきがえる hikigaeru

でんしゃ densha

キャンピングカー kyanpingu-kā

おか oka

23

ほしくさのやま
hoshikusa no yama

ぼくようけん
bokuyō-ken

あひる ahiru

こひつじ ko-hitsuji

いけ ike

ひよこ hiyoko

やねうら yane-ura

ぶたごや buta-goya

おうし o-ushi

あひるのこ ahiru no ko

にわとりごや
niwatori-goya

トラクター torakutā

のうじょう nōjō

おんどり ondori

がちょう gachō

タンクしゃ tanku-sha

なや naya

ぬかるみ
nukarumi

ておしぐるま
te-oshi-guruma

24

のうふ nôfu

そうげん sôgen

めんどり mendori

こうし ko-ushi

へい hei

サドル sadoru

うしごや ushi-goya

めうし me-ushi

すき suki

かじゅ kaju

うまごや uma-goya

こぶた ko-buta

ひつじかい hitsujikai

しちめんちょう shichimenchō

かかし kakashi

のうか nôka

ほしくさ hoshi-kusa

ひつじ hitsuji

わらたば wara-taba

うま uma

ぶた buta

25

はんせん hansen

うみ umi

オール ōru

とうだい tōdai

シャベル shaberu

バケツ baketsu

ひとで hitode

すなのしろ suna no shiro

ビーチパラソル
biichi-parasoru

はた hata

せんいん senin

うみべ umibe

かい kai

かに kani

かもめ kamome

しま shima

モーターボート
mōtā-bōto

すいじょうスキー
suijō-sukii

なみ nami

なつのぼうし natsu no bōshi

がけ gake

ふね fune

カヌー kanū

ロープ rōpu

こいし koishi

かいそう kaisō

あみ ami

みずかき mizu-kaki

つりぶね tsuri-bune

あしびれ ashi-bire

ろば roba

さかな sakana

みずぎ mizugi

オイルタンカー oiru-tankā

はまべ hamabe

ボート bōto

おりたたみいす oritatami-isu

27

はさみ hasami

2 + 2 = 4
3 + 2 = 5

けいさん keisan

けしごむ keshigomu

ものさし monosashi

しゃしん shashin

フェルトペン
fueruto-pen

がびょう gabyō

えのぐ enogu

おとこのこ otoko no ko

えんぴつ enpitsu

がっこう gakkō

こくばん kokuban

つくえ tsukue

ほん hon

ペン pen

のり nori

チョーク chōku

え e

ごみばこ
gomibako

せんせい sensei

はこ hako

ちず chizu

ふで fude

てんじょう tenjō

かべ kabe

ゆか yuka

ノート nōto

abcdefg
hijklmn
opqrstu
vwxyz
アルファベット
arufabetto

バッジ bajji

すいそう suisō

かみ kami

ブラインド buraindo

イーゼル iizeru

ドアのとって
doa no totte

しょくぶつ
shokubutsu

ちきゅうぎ
chikyūgi

おんなのこ
onna no ko

クレヨン kureyon

スタンド
sutando

イーゼル iizeru

29

かんごふ kangofu

だっしめん dasshimen

くすり kusuri

エレベーター erebētā

ガウン gaun

まつばづえ matsuba-zue

じょうざい jōzai

おぼん o-bon

うでとけい ude-dokei

たいおんけい taionkei

カーテン kāten

びょういん byōin

テディベア tedibea

りんご ringo

ギブス gibusu

ほうたい hōtai

くるまいす kuruma-isu

ジグゾーパズル jiguzō-pazuru

いしゃ isha

ちゅうしゃき chūshaki

いしゃ isha

スリッパ surippa

コンピューター konpyūtā

バンドエイド bando-eido

バナナ banana

ぶどう budō

かご kago

おもちゃ omocha

なし nashi

カード kādo

お-むつ omutsu

つえ tsue

テレビ terebi

ねまき nemaki

パジャマ pajama

オレンジ orenji

ティッシュ・ペーパー tisshu-pēpā

まんが manga

まちあいしつ machiai-shitsu

31

パーティー _{pātii}

プレゼント purezento

ふうせん fūsen

チョコレート
chokorēto

おかし okashi

まど mado

はなび hanabi

リボン ribon

ケーキ kēki

ストロー
sutorō

ろうそく
rōsoku

かみくさり kami-kusari

おもちゃ omocha

みかん mikan

サラミ sarami

カセットテープ
kasetto-tēpu

ソーセージ sōsēji

ポテトチップス
poteto-chippusu

かそうふく kasō-fuku

さくらんぼ sakuranbo

フルーツジュース
furūtsu-jūsu

きいちご ki-ichigo

いちご ichigo

でんきゅう denkyū

サンドウィッチ
sandoitchi

バター batā

クッキー
kukkii

チーズ chiizu

パン pan

テーブルクロス
tēburu-kurosu

33

グレープフルーツ
gurēpu-furūtsu

にんじん ninjin

カリフラワー
karifurawā

にら nira

マッシュルーム
masshurūmu

きゅうり kyūri

レモン remon

セロリ serori

アプリコット apurikotto

メロン meron

おみせ omise

かいものぶくろ
kaimono-bukuro

チーズ

くだもの と やさい

たまねぎ
tamanegi

キャベツ kyabetsu

もも momo

レタス retasu

さやえんどう
saya-endō

トマト tomato

たまご tamago

 プラム puramu

 こむぎこ komugiko

 はかり hakari

 びん bin

 にく niku

 パイン pain

 ヨーグルト yōguruto

 バスケット basuketto

 ボトル botoru

 ハンドバッグ hando-baggu

 さいふ saifu

 おかね o-kane

 かんづめ kanzume

 トロリー tororii

 じゃがいも jaga-imo

ほうれんそう hōrensō

いんげん ingen

 レジ reji

 かぼちゃ kabocha

35

たべもの tabemono

ひるごはん hiru-gohan

あさごはん asa-gohan

ゆでたまご yude-tamago

トースト tōsuto

ジャム jamu

コーヒー kōhii

めだまやき medama-yaki

コーンフレーク kōn-furēku

ココア kokoa

クリーム kuriimu

ぎゅうにゅう gyūnyū

はちみつ hachimitsu

こしょう koshō

しお shio

さとう satō

こうちゃ kōcha

ティーポット tiipotto

ホットケーキ hotto-kēki

ロールパン rōru-pan

ばんごはん ban-gohan

ハム hamu

スープ sūpu

オムレツ omuretsu

サラダ sarada

はし hashi

ハンバーガー hanbāgā

とりにく tori-niku

ごはん gohan

ソース sōsu

スパゲッティー supagettii

マッシュポテト masshu-poteto

ピザ piza

フライドポテト furaido-poteto

デザート dezāto

わたし watashi

あたま atama

かみ kami

かお kao

うで ude

ひじ hiji

おなか onaka

つまさき tsumasaki

あし ashi

あし ashi

ひざ hiza

まゆげ mayuge

め me

はな hana

ほほ hoho

くち kuchi

くちびる kuchibiru

は ha

した shita

あご ago

みみ mimi

くび kubi

かた kata

むね mune

せなか senaka

おしり oshiri

て te

おやゆび oya-yubi

ゆび yubi

38

わたしのようふく

ソックス sokkusu　パンツ pantsu　ランニングシャツ ranning-shatsu　ズボン zubon　ジーパン jiipan　ティーシャツ tiishatsu

スカート sukăto　シャツ shatsu　ネクタイ nekutai　はんズボン hanzubon　タイツ taitsu　ドレス doresu

ジャンパー janpă　トレーナー torēnă　カーディガン kădigan　スカーフ sukăfu　ハンカチ hankachi

スニーカー suniikă　くつ kutsu　サンダル sandaru　ブーツ bŭtsu　てぶくろ tebukuro

ベルト beruto　バックル bakkuru　ジッパー jippă　くつひも kutsuhimo　ボタン botan　ボタンのあな botan no ana

ポケット poketto　コート kŏto　ジャケット jaketto　やきゅうぼう yakyū-bŏ　ぼうし bŏshi

ひと hito

だんゆう danyū

じょゆう joyū

コック kokku

ダンサー dansā

かしゅ kashu

うちゅうひこうし
uchū-hikōshi

にくや nikuya

けいかん keikan

ふじんけいかん
fujin-keikan

だいく daiku

しょうぼうし
shōbōshi

がか gaka

さいばんかん saibankan

せいびし seibishi

トラックのうんてんしゅ torakku no untenshu

バスのうんてんしゅ basu no untenshu

びようし biyōshi

はいしゃ haisha

せんすいふ sensuifu

ゆうびんはいたつにん
yūbin-haitatsunin

ウェイター ueitá　ウェイトレス ueitoresu

ペンキや penkiya

パンや panya

かぞく kazoku

おば oba　おじ oji

そふ sofu

そぼ sobo

むすこ musuko　むすめ musume
おとうと otōto　あね ane

はは haha　ちち chichi
つま tsuma　おっと otto

いとこ itoko

41

どうさ dōsa

ほほえむ hohoemu

なく naku

かんがえる kangaeru

きく kiku

わらう warau

なげる nageru

こわす kowasu

えがく egaku

かく kaku

うけとる uketoru

たたききる tataki-kiru

きる kiru

たべる taberu

はなす hanasu

ほる horu

はこぶ hakobu

のむ nomu

つくる tsukuru

とぶ tobu

はう hau

おどる odoru

あらう arau

あむ amu

あそぶ asobu

みる miru

のぼる noboru

とる toru

はねる haneru

けんかする kenka-suru

ねる neru

ぬう nuu

まつ matsu

りょうりする ryōri-suru

かくれる kakureru

よむ yomu

かう kau

おす osu

うたう utau

ふく fuku

ひく hiku

はく haku

つむ tsumu

ころぶ korobu

あるく aruku

はしる hashiru

すわる suwaru

43

はんたいのことば
hantai no kotoba

よい yoi

わるい warui

いちばんうえ ichiban-ue

いちばんした ichiban-shita

ふとった futotta

やせた yaseta

すくない sukunai

おおい ōi

とおい tōi

ちかい chikai

つめたい tsumetai

あつい atsui

きたない kitanai

きれい kirei

あく aku

しまる shimaru

いちばん ichiban

さいご saigo

ぬれる nureru

かわいてる kawaiteru

うえ ue

した shita

ちいさい chiisai

おおきい ōkii

ひだり hidari

44

そと soto

なか naka

かんたん kantan

むずかしい muzukashii

から kara　　いっぱい ippai

やわらかい yawarakai

かたい katai

まえ mae

たかい takai

おそい osoi

はやい hayai

うしろ ushiro

ながい nagai

ひくい hikui

みじかい mijikai

かれた kareta　　さいている saiteiru

くらい kurai

あかるい akarui

ふるい furui

にかい nikai

みぎ migi

あたらしい atarashii

いっかい ikkai

いろいろな ひ iroirona-hi

げつようび getsu-yōbi

かようび ka-yōbi

すいようび sui-yōbi

もくようび moku-yōbi

きんようび kin-yōbi

どようび do-yōbi

にちようび nichi-yōbi

カレンダー karendā

あさ asa

ゆうがた yūgata

たいよう taiyō

よる yoru

つき tsuki

ほし hoshi

うちゅう uchū

わくせい wakusei

うちゅうせん uchū-sen

てんたいぼうえんきょう tentai-bōenkyō

とくべつなひ tokubetsuna-hi

たんじょうび
tanjōbi

たんじょうびのカード
tanjōbi no kādo

ろうそく rōsoku

きゅうか kyūka

プレゼント purezento

たんじょうびのケーキ
tanjōbi no kēki

けっこんしき kekkon-shiki

カメラ kamera

ブライズ・メイド
buraizu meido

はなよめ
hana-yome

はなむこ
hana-muko

カメラマン kamera-man

クリスマス kurisumasu

トナカイ
tonakai

そり sori

サンタクロース santa-kurōsu

クリスマスツリー
kurisumasu-tsurii

てんき tenki

かさ kasa

あめ ame

かみなり kaminari

かぜ kazo

かすみ kasumi

たいよう taiyō

くも kumo

そら sora

きり kiri

つゆ tsuyu

ゆき yuki

しも shimo

にじ niji

きせつ kisetsu

はる haru

なつ natsu

あき aki

ふゆ fuyu

48

ペット petto

ハムスター hamusutā

じゅうい jūi

いぬごや inu-goya

モルモット morumotto

こいぬ ko-inu

いぬ inu

てのりぶんちょう tenori-bunchō

おうむ ōmu

くちばし kuchibashi

えさ esa

カナリア kanaria

とりかご torikago

うさぎ usagi

ねこ neko

バスケット basuketto

こねこ ko-neko

ねずみ nezumi

ぎゅうにゅう gyūnyū

きんぎょ kingyo

スポーツとうんどう supōtsu to undō

ボートのり
bōto-nori

スノウボード sunō-bōdo

セーリング sēringu

ウィンドサーフィン
uindo-sāfin

バスケットボール
basuketto-bōru

クリケット
kuriketto

からて karate

ラケット
raketto

バット batto

ボール
bōru

テニス tenisu

たいそう taisō

アメリカンフットボール
amerikan-futtobōru

つりざお tsuri-zao

えさ esa

ダンス dansu

やきゅう yakyū

つり tsuri

ラグビー ragubii

とびこみ tobikomi

プール pūru

すいえい suiei

レース rēsu

アーチェリー ācherii

まと mato

ハングライダー hanguraidā

ヘルメット herumetto

ジョギング jogingu

じてんしゃ jitensha

ロッククライミング rokku-kuraimingu

じゅうどう jūdō

うま uma

こうま ko-uma

ロッカー rokkā

サッカー sakkā

じょうば jōba

こういしつ kōi-shitsu

バトミントン batominton

たっきゅう takkyū

スケートぐつ sukēto-gutsu

アイススケート aisu-sukēto

ストック sutokku

スキーリフト sukii-rifuto

スキーいた sukii-ita

スキー sukii

すもう sumō

51

いろ iro

だいだいいろ daidai-iro

みどり midori

くろ kuro

はいいろ hai-iro

あか aka

ちゃいろ cha-iro

しろ shiro

あお ao

ピンク pinku

むらさき murasaki

きいろ ki-iro

かたち katachi

ちょうほうけい chōhōkei

えん en

ひしがた hishigata

コーン kōn

ほし hoshi

りっぽうたい rippōtai

だえんけい daenkei

さんかくけい sankakukei

せいほうけい seihōkei

みかづき mikazuki

かず kazu

1	いち ichi
2	に ni
3	さん san
4	し shi
5	ご go
6	ろく roku
7	しち shichi
8	はち hachi
9	きゅう kyū
10	じゅう jū
11	じゅういち jūichi
12	じゅうに jūni
13	じゅうさん jūsan
14	じゅうし jūshi
15	じゅうご jūgo
16	じゅうろく jūroku
17	じゅうしち jūshichi
18	じゅうはち jūhachi
19	じゅうきゅう jūkyū
20	にじゅう nijū

ゆうえんち yūenchi

メリーゴーランド
merii-gō-rando

マット
matto

すべりだい suberidai

かんらんしゃ kanransha

おばけやしき obake-yashiki

ポップコーン poppu-kō

わなげ wanage

ジェットコースター jetto-kōsutā

しゃげき shageki

ゴーカート gō-kāto

わたあめ wata-ame

サーカス sākasu

つなわたり tsunawatari

ポール pōru

くうちゅうブランコ kuchū-buranko

ワイヤーロープ waiyā-rōpu

いちりんしゃのり ichirinsha-nori

なわばしご nawabashigo

あんぜんネット anzen-netto

アクロバット akurobatto

きょくげいし kyokugeishi

フープ fūpu

ちょうきょうし chōkyōshi

いぬ inu

うさぎ usagi

シルクハット shiruku-hatto

ちょうねくたい chō-nekutai

バンド bando

うまのり umanori

ピエロ piero

Word list

In this list, you can find all the Japanese words in the book. For each double page, the Japanese words are shown in our alphabet, and next to each one you can see its English translation.

The translations match the pictures, so if the picture shows leaves, the translation is "leaves", not "leaf". In Japanese, though, there is usually no difference between singular and plural (one and many), so "leaf" and "leaves" are both "ha".

To know how you should say the Japanese words, look at page 2.

pages 4-5

uchi	home
yokushitsu	bathroom
ima	living room
shinshitsu	bedroom
genkan	hall
ofuro	bathtub
sekken	soap
jaguchi	faucet
toiretto-pēpā	toilet paper
ha-burashi	toothbrush
mizu	water
toire	toilet
suponji	sponge
senmendai	sink
shawā	shower
taoru	towel
hamigakiko	toothpaste
rajio	radio
kusshon	cushion
shiidii	CD
jūtan	carpet
sofā	sofa
rajiētā	radiator
bideo	video
shinbun	newspaper
tēburu	table
tegami	letters
kaidan	stairs
denwa	telephone
bōshi-kake	hat pegs
e	pictures
ranpu	lamp
burashi	brush
kagami	mirror
tansu	chest of drawers
makura	pillow
yōfuku-dansu	wardrobe
shikimono	rug
shiitsu	sheet
kushi	comb
kakebuton	comforter
isu	chair
beddo	bed

pages 6-7

daidokoro	kitchen
reizōko	refrigerator
koppu	cups
tokei	clock
koshikake	stool
kosaji	teaspoons
suitchi	light switch
senzai	laundry detergent
kagi	key
doa	door
denki-sōjiki	vacuum cleaner
nabe	saucepans
fōku	forks
epuron	apron
airon-dai	ironing board
gomi	trash
fukin	dish towel
kōhii-kappu	coffee cups
matchi	matches
tawashi	scrub brush
owan	bowls
shokki-dana	cupboard
airon	iron
osara	plates
supūn	spoons
renji	stove
furaipan	frying pan
ukezara	saucers
hikidashi	drawer
chiritori	dustpan
sentakuki	washing machine
hōki	broom
tairu	tiles
hataki	dust cloth
moppu	mop
naifu	knives
yakan	kettle
nagashi	sink

pages 8-9

niwa	yard
te-oshi-ichirinsha	wheelbarrow
mitsubachi no su	beehive
katatsumuri	snail

renga	bricks
hato	pigeon
suki	spade
tentō-mushi	ladybug
gomi-ire	trash can
tane	seeds
koya	shed
mimizu	worm
hana	flowers
supurinkurā	sprinkler
kuwa	hoe
suzume-bachi	wasp
kusa	grass
ubaguruma	baby buggy
hashigo	ladder
takibi	bonfire
hōsu	hose
onshitsu	greenhouse
bō	sticks
tori no su	bird's nest
kumade	rake
kemushi	caterpillar
kemuri	smoke
ki	tree
ha	leaves
ko-michi	path
shibakariki	lawn mower
mataguwa	fork
kakine	hedge
hone	bone
shaberu	trowel
mitsubachi	bee
jōro	watering can

pages 10-11

sagyōba	workshop
manriki	vice
kami-yasuri	sandpaper
doriru	drill
hashigo	ladder
nokogiri	saw
ogakuzu	sawdust
karendā	calendar
dogū-bako	tool box
sukuryū-doraibā	screwdriver

ita	plank
kanna-kuzu	wood shavings
pen-naifu	penknife
zaimoku	wood
kugi	nails
sagyōdai	workbench
bin	jars
kanna	wood plane
kan-penki	paint can
yasuri	file
hanmā	hammer
makijaku	tape measure
ono	axe
hae	fly
taru	barrel
kumo no su	cobweb
oya-neji	nuts
boruto	bolts
kumo	spider
byō	tacks
neji	screws

pages 12-13

tōri	street
mise	store
ana	hole
kissaten	café
kyūkyūsha	ambulance
hodō	pavement
antena	antenna
entotsu	chimney
yane	roof
shunsetsuki	digger
hoteru	hotel
otoko	man
patokā	police car
paipu	pipes
doriru	drill
gakkō	school
undō-jō	playground
jitensha	bicycle
shōbō-sha	fire engine
keikan	policeman
kuruma	car
onna	woman

gaitō	lamp post
apāto	apartments
ōtobai	motorcycle
fumidan	steps
ichiba	market
ie	house
tōrerā	trailer
rōrā	steamroller
raito-ban	van
eiga-kan	movie theater
kōtsū-shingō	traffic lights
torakku	truck
kōjō	factory
ōdan-hodō	crosswalk
takushii	taxi
basu	bus

pages 14-15

omochaya / toy shop

omochaya	toy shop
kisha-setto	train set
saikoro	dice
rekōdā	recorder
robotto	robot
doramu	drums
nekkuresu	necklace
kamera	camera
biizu	beads
ningyō	dolls
gitā	guitar
yubiwa	ring
ningyō no ie	doll's house
fue	whistle
tsumiki	blocks
o-shiro	castle
sensuikan	submarine
toranpetto	trumpet
ya	arrows
kurēn	crane
nendo	clay
teppō	gun
heitai	soldiers
enogu	paints
roketto	rocket
uchū-hikōshi	spacemen
piano	piano

ayatsuri-ningyō	puppets
bii-dama	marbles
chokin-bako	money box
mokuba	rocking horse
rēshingu-kā	racing car
omen	masks
rōrā	steamroller
fueisu-peinto	face paints
bōto	boat
parashūto	parachute
yumi	bow
hāmonika	harmonica

pages 16-17

kōen / park

kōen	park
buranko	swings
sunaba	sandbox
pikunikku	picnic
tako	kite
aisukuriimu	ice cream
inu	dog
mon	gate
ko-michi	path
kaeru	frog
suberidai	slide
otamajakushi	tadpoles
ike	lake
rōrā-sukēto	roller skates
yabu	bush
kadan	flower bed
hakuchō	swans
hikihimo	dog leash
kamo	ducks
ki	trees
nawatobi	jump rope
ko-gamo	ducklings
mizu-tamari	puddle
ito	string
yotto	toy boat
mari	ball
saku	fence
tori	birds
sanrinsha	tricycle
kodomo	children
shiisō	seesaw

te-oshi-guruma	stroller
tsuchi	dirt
sukētobōdo	skateboard
akanbō	baby
benchi	bench

pages 18-19

dōbutsuen / zoo

dōbutsuen	zoo
panda	panda
washi	eagle
tsubasa	wing
kaba	hippopotamus
saru	monkey
shippo	tail
kōmori	bat
gorira	gorilla
kangarū	kangaroo
mae-ashi	(front) paws
ōkami	wolf
wani	crocodile
pengin	penguin
hyōzan	iceberg
kuma	bear
perikan	pelican
dachō	ostrich
hane	feathers
iruka	dolphin
raion	lion
yōjū	cubs
kirin	giraffe
shika	deer
tsuno	horns
rakuda	camel
azarashi	seal
kame	tortoise
zō	elephant
zō no hana	trunk (elephant)
shiro-kuma	polar bear
sai	rhinoceros
yagyū	buffalo
biibā	beaver
yagi	goat
shima-uma	zebra
hebi	snake
same	shark

kujira	whale	yane-ura	loft
tora	tiger	buta-goya	pigsty
hyō	leopard	o-ushi	bull
		ahiru no ko	ducklings
		niwatori-goya	hen house
pages 20-21		torakutā	tractor
ryokō	**travel**	gachō	geese
eki	**station**	tanku-sha	tanker
gasorin-sutando	**gas station**	naya	barn
hikōjō	**airport**	nukarumi	mud
senro	train track	te-oshi-guruma	cart
enjin	engine	hoshi-kusa	hay
kanshōki	buffers	hitsuji	sheep
kyakusha	railway cars	wara-taba	straw bales
untenshu	train engineer	uma	horse
kasha	freight train	buta	pigs
puratto-hōmu	platform	nōka	farmhouse
shashō	ticket inspector	kakashi	scarecrow
sūtsukēsu	suitcase	shichimenchō	turkeys
jōshaken-hanbaiki	ticket machine	hitsujikai	shepherdess
shingō	signals	ko-buta	piglets
ryukkusakku	backpack	uma-goya	stable
heddo-raito	headlights	kaju	orchard
enjin	engine	suki	plow
sharin	wheel	me-ushi	cow
denchi	battery	ushi-goya	cowshed
gasorin-tankurōrii	oil tanker	sadoru	saddle
supana	wrench	hei	fence
taiya	tire	ko-ushi	calf
bonnetto	hood (car)	mendori	hens
oiru	oil	sōgen	field
gasorin-ponpu	gas pump	nōfu	farmer
rekkā-sha	tow truck	ondori	rooster
gasorin	gasoline		
toranku	trunk (car)		
sensha	car wash	**pages 26-27**	
pairotto	pilot	**umibe**	**seaside**
suchuwādo	flight attendant (man)	hansen	sailboat
		umi	sea
kanseitō	control tower	ōru	oar
kassōro	runway	tōdai	lighthouse
suchuwādesu	flight attendant (woman)	shaberu	shovel
		baketsu	bucket
hikōki	plane	hitode	starfish
herikoputā	helicopter	suna no shiro	sandcastle
		biichi-parasoru	umbrella

pages 22-23

inaka	**country**
fūsha-goya	windmill
netsu-kikyū	hot-air balloon
chō-cho	butterfly
tokage	lizard
ishi	stones
kitsune	fox
ogawa	stream
michi-shirube	signpost
hari-nezumi	hedgehog
sui-mon	canal
risu	squirrel
mori	forest
anaguma	badger
kawa	river
michi	road
iwa	rocks
hikigaeru	toad
densha	train
kyanpingu-kā	camper
oka	hill
tsuri-bito	fisherman
mogura	mole
kogitsune	fox cubs
tonneru	tunnel
fukurō	owl
taki	waterfall
hashike	barge
hashi	bridge
ga	moth
mura	village
maruta	logs
unga	canal
tento	tents
yama	mountain

pages 24-25

nōjō	**farm**
hoshikusa no yama	haystack
bokuyō-ken	sheepdog
ahiru	ducks
ko-hitsuji	lambs
ike	pond
hiyoko	chicks

hata	flag	e	drawing	nemaki	nightgown
senin	sailor	doa no totte	door handle	pajama	pajamas
kani	crab	shokubutsu	plant	orenji	orange
kamome	seagull	chikyūgi	globe	tisshu-pēpā	tissues
shima	island	onna no ko	girl	manga	comic
mōtā-bōto	motorboat	kureyon	crayons	machiai-shitsu	waiting room
suijō-sukii	water skiing	sutando	lamp	tsue	cane
mizugi	swimsuit	iizeru	easel	omutsu	diaper
oiru-tankā	oil tanker	buraindo	blind	kādo	cards
hamabe	beach	kami	paper	nashi	pear
bōto	rowboat	suisō	aquarium	omocha	toys
oritatami-isu	deck chair	bajji	badge	kago	basket
sakana	fish	arufabetto	alphabet	budō	grapes
roba	donkey	nōto	notebook	banana	banana
ashi-bire	flippers	yuka	floor	bando-eido	bandaid
tsuri-bune	fishing boat	kabe	wall	konpyūtā	computer
mizu-kaki	paddle	tenjō	ceiling	surippa	slippers
ami	net	fude	paint brush	ringo	apple
kaisō	seaweed	chizu	map	tedibea	teddy bear
koishi	pebbles	hako	box		
rōpu	rope	sensei	teacher		
kanū	canoe	gomibako	wastepaper basket	**pages 32-33**	
fune	ship	kokuban	board	**pātii**	**party**
gake	cliff			fūsen	balloon
natsu no bōshi	sunhat			chokorēto	chocolate
nami	waves	**pages 30-31**		okashi	candy
kai	shell	**byōin**	**hospital**	mado	window
		isha	**doctor**	hanabi	fireworks
		kangofu	nurse	ribon	ribbon
pages 28-29		dasshimen	cotton	kēki	cake
gakkō	**school**	kusuri	medicine	sutorō	straw
hasami	scissors	erebētā	elevator	rōsoku	candle
keisan	calculation	gaun	bathrobe	kami-kusari	paper chains
keshigomu	eraser	matsuba-zue	crutches	omocha	toys
monosashi	ruler	jōzai	pills	sandoitchi	sandwich
shashin	photographs	o-bon	tray	batā	butter
fueruto-pen	felt-tip pens	ude-dokei	watch	kukkii	cookie
gabyō	thumb tacks	taionkei	thermometer	chiizu	cheese
enogu	paints	kāten	curtain	pan	bread
otoko no ko	boy	gibusu	cast	tēburu-kurosu	tablecloth
enpitsu	pencil	hōtai	bandage	denkyū	light bulb
tsukue	desk	kuruma-isu	wheelchair	ichigo	strawberry
hon	books	jiguzō-pazuru	jigsaw puzzle	ki-ichigo	raspberry
pen	pen	isha	doctor	furūtsu-jūsu	fruit juice
nori	glue	chūshaki	syringe	sakuranbo	cherry
chōku	chalk	terebi	television	kasō-fuku	costume

poteto-chippusu	potato chips
sōsēji	sausage
kasetto-tēpu	cassette tape
sarami	salami
mikan	tangerine
purezento	presents

pages 34-35

omise	**grocery store**
gurēpu-furūtsu	grapefruit
ninjin	carrot
karifurawā	cauliflower
nira	leek
masshurūmu	mushroom
kyūri	cucumber
remon	lemon
serori	celery
apurikotto	apricot
meron	melon
tamanegi	onion
kyabetsu	cabbage
momo	peach
retasu	lettuce
saya-endō	peas
tomato	tomato
jaga-imo	potatoes
hōrensō	spinach
ingen	beans
reji	checkout
kabocha	pumpkin
tororii	shopping cart
kanzume	cans
o-kane	money
saifu	coin purse
hando-baggu	purse
botoru	bottles
basuketto	basket
yōguruto	yogurt
pain	pineapple
niku	meat
bin	jars
hakari	scales
komugiko	flour
puramu	plum
tamago	eggs

kaimono-bukuro	carrier bag
chiizu	cheese
kudamono	fruit
yasai	vegetables

pages 36-37

tabemono	**food**
asa-gohan	breakfast
hiru-gohan	lunch
yude-tamago	boiled egg
kōhii	coffee
medama-yaki	fried egg
tōsuto	toast
jamu	jam
kuriimu	cream
gyūnyū	milk
kōn-furēku	cornflakes
kokoa	hot chocolate
satō	sugar
hachimitsu	honey
shio	salt
koshō	pepper
kōcha	tea
tiipotto	teapot
hotto-kēki	pancakes
rōru-pan	rolls
ban-gohan	supper
hamu	ham
sūpu	soup
omuretsu	omelette
hashi	chopsticks
sarada	salad
hanbāgā	hamburger
tori-niku	chicken
gohan	rice
sōsu	sauce
supagettii	spaghetti
masshu-poteto	mashed potatoes
piza	pizza
furaido-poteto	french fries
dezāto	dessert

pages 38-39

watashi	**me, I**
atama	head
kami	hair
kao	face
ude	arm
hiji	elbow
onaka	tummy
ashi	leg
tsumasaki	toes
ashi	foot
hiza	knee
mayuge	eyebrow
me	eye
hana	nose
hoho	cheek
kuchi	mouth
kuchibiru	lips
ha	teeth
shita	tongue
ago	chin
mimi	ears
kubi	neck
kata	shoulders
mune	chest
senaka	back
oshiri	bottom
te	hand
oya-yubi	thumb
yubi	fingers
watashi no yōfuku	**my clothes**
sokkusu	socks
pantsu	underwear
ranning-shatsu	undershirt
zubon	pants
jiipan	jeans
tiishatsu	T-shirt
sukāto	skirt
shatsu	shirt
nekutai	tie
hanzubon	shorts
taitsu	tights
doresu	dress
janpā	sweater
torēnā	sweatshirt
kādigan	cardigan

sukāfu	scarf			toru	take
hankachi	handkerchief			kenka-suru	fight
suniikā	sneakers			neru	sleep
kutsu	shoes			nuu	sew
sandaru	sandals			haneru	skip
būtsu	boots			matsu	wait
tebukuro	gloves			ryōri-suru	cook
beruto	belt			kakureru	hide
bakkuru	buckle			yomu	read
jippā	zipper			kau	buy
kutsuhimo	shoelace			utau	sing
botan	buttons			osu	push
botan no ana	button holes			haku	sweep
poketto	pockets			tsumu	pick
kōto	coat			fuku	blow
jaketto	jacket			hiku	pull
yakyū-bō	baseball cap			korobu	fall
bōshi	hat			aruku	walk
				hashiru	run
				suwaru	sit

kazoku — **families**

musuko	son
otōto	younger brother
ani	older brother
musume	daughter
ane	older sister
imōto	younger sister
haha	mother
tsuma	wife
chichi	father
otto	husband
oba	aunt
oji	uncle
itoko	cousin
sofu	grandfather
sobo	grandmother

pages 40-41

hito — **people**

danyū	actor
joyū	actress
kokku	chef
dansā	dancers
kashu	singers
nikuya	butcher
keikan	policeman
fujin-keikan	policewoman
uchū-hikōshi	astronaut
daiku	carpenter
shōbōshi	firefighter
gaka	artist
saibankan	judge
seibishi	mechanics
biyōshi	barber
torakku no untenshu	truck driver
basu no untenshu	bus driver
haisha	dentist
sensuifu	frogman
ueitā	waiter
ueitoresu	waitress
yūbin-haitatsunin	mail carrier
penkiya	painter
panya	baker

pages 42-43

dōsa — **doing things**

warau	laugh
hohoemu	smile
naku	cry
kangaeru	think
kiku	listen
uketoru	catch
nageru	throw
kowasu	break
egaku	paint
kaku	write
tataki-kiru	chop
kiru	cut
taberu	eat
hanasu	talk
horu	dig
hakobu	carry
nomu	drink
tsukuru	make
tobu	jump
hau	crawl
odoru	dance
arau	wash
amu	knit
asobu	play
miru	watch
noboru	climb

pages 44-45

hantai no kotoba — **opposite words**

tōi	far
chikai	near
yoi	good
warui	bad
tsumetai	cold
atsui	hot
nureru	wet
kawaiteru	dry
ichiban-ue	top
ichiban-shita	bottom
kitanai	dirty
kirei	clean
ue	over
shita	under
futotta	fat
yaseta	thin
aku	open
shimaru	closed
chiisai	small
ōkii	big
sukunai	few
ōi	many

ichiban	first	wakusei	planet	hamusutā	hamster
saigo	last	tsuki	moon	morumotto	guinea pig
hidari	left	hoshi	star	inu-goya	kennel
migi	right	tentai-bōenkyō	telescope	ko-inu	puppy
soto	out	**tokubetsuna-hi**	**special days**	inu	dog
naka	in	tanjōbi	birthday	esa	food
kantan	easy	purezento	present	tenori-bunchō	parakeet
muzukashii	difficult	tanjōbi no kēki	birthday cake	ōmu	parrot
kara	empty	rōsoku	candle	kuchibashi	beak
ippai	full	tanjōbi no kādo	birthday card	usagi	rabbit
yawarakai	soft	kyūka	vacation	kanaria	canary
katai	hard	kekkon-shiki	wedding day	torikago	bird cage
mae	front	buraizu meido	bridesmaid	neko	cat
ushiro	back	hana-yome	bride	basuketto	basket
takai	high	hana-muko	bridegroom	nezumi	mouse
hikui	low	kamera-man	photographer	ko-neko	kitten
osoi	slow	kamera	camera	gyūnyū	milk
hayai	fast	kurisumasu	Christmas Day	kingyo	goldfish
nagai	long	santa-kurōsu	Santa Claus		
mijikai	short	sori	sleigh		
kareta	dead	kurisumasu-tsurii	Christmas tree		
saiteiru	alive	tonakai	reindeer		
kurai	dark				
akarui	light				

pages 50-51

supōtsu to undō	**sports & exercise**
basuketto-bōru	basketball
bōto-nori	rowing
sunō-bōdo	snowboarding
sēringu	sailing
uindo-sāfin	windsurfing
raketto	racket
tenisu	tennis
amerikan-futtobōru	American football
taisō	gym
kuriketto	cricket (sport)
karate	karate
tsuri-zao	fishing rod
tsuri	fishing
esa	bait
ragubii	rugby
dansu	dance
yakyū	baseball
bōru	ball
batto	bat
tobikomi	diving
pūru	swimming pool
suiei	swimming
rēsu	race
ācherii	archery

furui	old
atarashii	new
nikai	upstairs
ikkai	downstairs

pages 46-47

iroirona-hi	**days**
getsu-yōbi	Monday
ka-yōbi	Tuesday
sui-yōbi	Wednesday
moku-yōbi	Thursday
kin-yōbi	Friday
do-yōbi	Saturday
nichi-yōbi	Sunday
karendā	calendar
asa	morning
taiyō	sun
yūgata	evening
yoru	night
uchū	space
uchū-sen	spaceship

pages 48-49

tenki	**weather**
kasa	umbrella
ame	rain
kaminari	lightning
kiri	fog
yuki	snow
tsuyu	dew
sora	sky
taiyō	sun
kumo	clouds
kaze	wind
kasumi	mist
shimo	frost
niji	rainbow
kisetsu	**seasons**
haru	spring
natsu	summer
aki	autumn
fuyu	winter
petto	**pets**
jūi	vet

mato	target	seihōkei	square	anzen-netto	safety net
hanguraidā	hang-gliding	mikazuki	crescent	kyokugeishi	juggler
jogingu	jogging	**kazu**	**numbers**	fūpu	hoop
jūdō	judo	ichi	one	chōkyōshi	ring master
jitensha	cycling	ni	two	inu	dog
rokku-kuraimingu	climbing	san	three	usagi	rabbit
herumetto	helmet	shi	four	shiruku-hatto	top hat
batominton	badminton	go	five	bando	band
sakkā	soccer	roku	six	umanori	bareback rider
jōba	riding	shichi	seven	chō-nekutai	bowtie
uma	horse	hachi	eight	piero	clown
ko-uma	pony	kyū	nine		
kōi-shitsu	changing room	jū	ten		
rokkā	locker	jūichi	eleven		
takkyū	table tennis	jūni	twelve		
aisu-sukēto	ice skating	jūsan	thirteen		
sukēto-gutsu	ice skates	jūshi	fourteen		
sukii	skiing	jūgo	fifteen		
sutokku	ski pole	jūroku	sixteen		
sukii-ita	ski	jūshichi	seventeen		
sukii-rifuto	chairlift	jūhachi	eighteen		
sumō	sumo wrestling	jūkyū	nineteen		
		nijū	twenty		

pages 52-53

iro	**colors**
daidai-iro	orange
midori	green
kuro	black
hai-iro	grey
aka	red
cha-iro	brown
shiro	white
ao	blue
pinku	pink
murasaki	purple
ki-iro	yellow
katachi	**shapes**
chōhōkei	rectangle
en	circle
hishigata	diamond
kōn	cone
hoshi	star
rippōtai	cube
daenkei	oval
sankakukei	triangle

pages 54-55

yūenchi	**fairground**
kanransha	Ferris wheel
merii-gō-rando	merry-go-round
suberidai	slide
matto	mat
wanage	ring toss
obake-yashiki	haunted house ride
poppu-kōn	popcorn
jetto-kōsutā	roller coaster
shageki	rifle range
gō-kāto	bumper cars
wata-ame	cotton candy
sākasu	**circus**
ichirinsha-nori	unicyclist
akurobatto	acrobats
kuchū-buranko	trapeze
nawabashigo	rope ladder
tsunawatari	tightrope walker
pōru	pole
waiyā-rōpu	tightrope

This revised edition first published in 1995 by Usborne Publishing Ltd, Usborne House, 83-85 Saffron Hill, London EC1N 8RT.
Based on a previous title first published in 1979.
Copyright © 1995, 1979 Usborne Publishing Ltd.
First published in America in March 1996.

Printed in Italy.